HORRID HENRY
Tricks and Treats

HORRiD HENRY
Tricks and Treats

Francesca Simon
Illustrated by Tony Ross

Orion
Children's Books

Horrid Henry Tricks and Treats originally appeared in
Horrid Henry and the Bogey Babysitter first published in Great Britain in
2002 by Orion Children's Books
This edition first published in Great Britain in 2011
by Orion Children's Books
a division of the Orion Publishing Group Ltd
Orion House
5 Upper Saint Martin's Lane
London WC2H 9EA
An Hachette UK Company

3 5 7 9 10 8 6 4 2

Text © Francesca Simon 2002, 2011
Illustrations © Tony Ross 2011

Printed in China.

www.orionbooks.co.uk
www.horridhenry.co.uk

For the divine
Alice Burden

Look out for . . .

Don't Be Horrid, Henry!
Horrid Henry's Birthday Party
Horrid Henry's Holiday
Horrid Henry's Underpants
Horrid Henry Gets Rich Quick
Horrid Henry and the Football Fiend
Horrid Henry's Nits
Horrid Henry and Moody Margaret
Horrid Henry's Thank You Letter
Horrid Henry Reads A Book
Horrid Henry's Car Journey
Moody Margaret's School

There are many more **Horrid Henry** books
available. For a complete list visit
www.horridhenry.co.uk

or

www.orionbooks.co.uk

Contents

Chapter 1

Hallowe'en!
Oh happy, happy day!

Every year Horrid Henry could not believe it: an entire day devoted to stuffing your face with sweets and playing horrid tricks. Best of all, you were *supposed* to stuff your face and play horrid tricks.

Whoopee!

Horrid Henry was armed and ready.
He had loo roll.
He had water pistols.
He had shaving foam.
Oh my, would he be playing
tricks tonight.

Anyone who didn't instantly hand over a fistful of sweets would get it with the foam.

And **woe betide** any fool who gave him an apple. Horrid Henry knew how to treat rotten grown-ups like that.

His red and black devil costume
lay ready on the bed, complete
with evil mask, twinkling horns,
trident, and whippy tail.
He'd scare everyone wearing that.
"Heh heh heh," said Horrid Henry,
practising his evil laugh.

"Henry," came a little voice outside his bedroom door, "come and see my new costume."

"No," said Henry. "I'm busy."

16

"You're just jealous because *my* costume is nicer than yours," said Peter.

"Am not."

"Are too."

Come to think of it, what *was* Peter wearing?

Last year he'd copied Henry's
monster costume and ruined
Henry's Hallowe'en.

What if he were copying Henry's
devil costume? That would be just
like that horrible little copycat.
"All right, you can come in for
two seconds," said Henry.

A big, pink, bouncy bunny
bounded into Henry's room.
It had little white bunny ears.
It had a little white bunny tail.
It had pink polka dots
everywhere else.

Horrid Henry groaned.
What a stupid costume.
Thank goodness he wasn't
wearing it.

"Isn't it great?" said Perfect Peter.

"No," said Henry. "It's horrible."

"You're just saying that to
be mean, Henry," said Peter,
bouncing up and down.
"I can't wait to go trick-or-treating
in it tonight."

Chapter 2

Oh no.

Horrid Henry felt as if he'd been punched in the stomach.

Henry would be expected to go out
trick-or-treating . . . with Peter!
He, Henry, would have to walk
around with a pink polka dot bunny.
Everyone would see him.
The shame of it!

Rude Ralph would never stop
teasing him. Moody Margaret
would call him a bunny wunny.
How could he play tricks on people
with a pink polka dot bunny
following him everywhere?
He was ruined.
His name would be a joke.

"You can't wear that,"
said Henry desperately.

"Yes I can," said Peter.

"I won't let you," said Henry.

Perfect Peter looked at Henry.
"You're just jealous."

Grrr!

Horrid Henry was about to tear
that stupid costume off Peter when,
suddenly, he had an idea.

It was painful.
It was humiliating.

But anything was better than having
Peter prancing about in pink
polka dots.

Chapter 3

"Tell you what," said Henry,
"just because I'm so nice I'll let you
borrow my monster costume.
You've always wanted to wear it."

"NO!" said Peter.
"I want to be a bunny."

"But you're supposed to be scary for
Hallowe'en," said Henry.

"I am scary," said Peter.
"I'm going to bounce up to people
and yell 'boo'."

"I can make you really scary, Peter,"
said Horrid Henry.

"How?" said Peter.

"Sit down and I'll show you."
Henry patted his desk chair.

"What are you going to do?"
said Peter suspiciously.
He took a step back.

"Nothing," said Henry.
"I'm just trying to help you."

Perfect Peter didn't move.
"How can I be scarier?"
he said cautiously.

"I can give you a scary haircut,"
said Henry.

Perfect Peter clutched his curls.
"But I like my hair," he said feebly.

"This is Hallowe'en," said Henry.
"Do you want to be scary
or don't you?"

"Um, um, uh," said Peter,
as Henry pushed him down in
the chair and got out the scissors.

"Not too much," squealed Peter.

"Of course not," said Horrid Henry.
"Just sit back and relax,
I promise you'll love this."

Horrid Henry twirled the scissors.

Snip! Snip! Snip!
Snip! Snip!

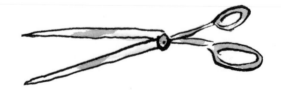

Chapter 4

Magnificent, thought Horrid Henry.
He gazed proudly at his work.

Maybe he should be a hairdresser when he grew up. Yes! Henry could see it now. Customers would queue for miles for one of Monsieur Henri's scary snips.

Shame his genius was wasted on someone as yucky as Peter. Still . . .

"You look great, Peter," said Henry.
"Really scary. Atomic Bunny.
Go and have a look."

Peter went over and looked
in the mirror.

"AAAAAAAAAARGGGGGGG!"

"Scared yourself, did you?"
said Henry. "That's great."

"AAAAAAAAAARGGGGGGG!"

howled Peter.

Mum ran into the room.

"AAAAAAAAAARGGGGGGG!"
howled Mum.

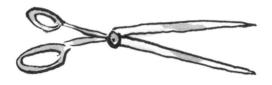

"AAAAAAAAAARGGGGGGG!"
howled Peter.

"Henry!" screeched Mum.
"What have you done?!
You horrid, horrid boy!"

What was left of Peter's hair stuck up in **ragged** tufts all over his head.

On one side was a
big bald patch.

"I was just making him look scary," protested Henry. "He said I could."

"Henry made me!" said Peter.

"My poor baby," said Mum.
She glared at Henry.

"No trick-or-treating for you,"
said Mum. "You'll stay here."

Horrid Henry could hardly believe
his ears. This was the worst thing
that had ever happened to him.

"NO!"

howled Henry.
This was all Peter's fault.
"I hate you, Peter!" he screeched.

Then he attacked.
He was Medusa, coiling round
her victim with her snaky hair.

"Aaaahh!"

screeched Peter.

"Henry!" shouted Mum.
"Go to your room!"

Chapter 5

Mum and Peter left the house to go
trick-or-treating.

Henry had screamed and sobbed and begged. He'd put on his devil costume, just in case his tears melted their stony hearts.

But no.

His mean, horrible parents
wouldn't change their mind.
Well, they'd be sorry.
They'd all be sorry.

Dad came into the sitting room.
He was holding a large shopping bag.
"Henry, I've got some work to finish
so I'm going to let you hand out
treats to any trick-or-treaters."

Horrid Henry stopped plotting
his revenge. Had Dad gone mad?
Hand out treats?
What kind of punishment was this?
Horrid Henry fought to keep
a big smile off his face.

"Here's the Hallowe'en stuff,
Henry," said Dad.
He handed Henry the heavy bag.
"But remember," he added sternly,
"these treats are not for you:
they're to give away."

Yeah, right,
thought Henry.

"OK, Dad," he said as meekly
as he could. "Whatever you say."
Dad went back to the kitchen.

Now was his chance!
Horrid Henry leapt on the bag.
Wow, was it full! He'd grab all the
good stuff, throw back anything
yucky with lime or peppermint,
and he'd have enough sweets to keep
him going for at least a week!

Henry yanked open the bag.
A terrible sight met his eyes.

The bag was full of satsumas.
And apples.
And walnuts in their shells.

No wonder his horrible parents
had trusted him to be in charge of it.

Ding dong.

Slowly, Horrid Henry heaved his
heavy bones to the door.
There was his empty, useless trick-
or-treat bag, sitting forlornly by the
entrance. Henry gave it a kick,
then opened the door and glared.

"Whaddya want?"
snapped Horrid Henry.

"Trick or treat,"
whispered Weepy William.
He was dressed as a pirate.

Horrid Henry held out
the bag of horrors.
"Lucky dip!" he announced.
"Close your eyes for a big surprise!"
William certainly would be surprised
at what a rotten treat he'd be getting.

Weepy William put down
his swag bag, closed his eyes tight,
then plunged his hand into
Henry's lucky dip.
He rummaged and he rummaged
and he rummaged, hoping to find
something better than satsumas.

Horrid Henry eyed Weepy William's
bulging swag bag.

Go on, Henry, urged the bag.
He'll never notice.

Horrid Henry did not wait
to be asked twice.

Dip!
Zip!
Pop!

Horrid Henry grabbed a big handful
of William's sweets and popped them
inside his empty bag.

Weepy William opened his eyes.
"Did you take some of my sweets?"

"No," said Henry.

William peeked inside his bag
and burst into tears.
"Waaaaaaaa!" wailed William.
"Henry took . . ."

Henry pushed him out
and slammed the door.

Dad came running.
"What's wrong?"

"Nothing," said Henry.
"Just William crying 'cause he's
scared of pumpkins."

Phew, thought Henry.
That was close. Perhaps he had been
a little too greedy.

Chapter 6

Ding dong.

It was Lazy Linda wearing
a pillowcase over her head.
Gorgeous Gurinder was with her,
dressed as a scarecrow.

"Trick or treat!"
"Trick or treat!"

"Close your eyes for a big surprise!"
said Henry, holding out
the lucky dip bag.

"Ooh, a lucky dip!" squealed Linda.

Lazy Linda and Gorgeous Gurinder
put down their bags, closed their
eyes, and reached into the lucky dip.

Dip!

Zip!

Pop!

Dip!

Zip!

Pop!

Lazy Linda opened her eyes.
"You give the worst treats ever,
Henry," said Linda, gazing at her
walnut in disgust.

"We won't be coming back *here*,"
sniffed Gorgeous Gurinder.

Tee hee, thought Horrid Henry.

Ding dong.

It was Beefy Bert.
He was wearing a robot costume.

"Hi, Bert, got any good sweets?"
asked Henry.

"I dunno," said Beefy Bert.

Horrid Henry soon found out
that he did.

Lots and lots and lots
of them.

So did Moody Margaret,

Sour Susan,

Jolly Josh

and Tidy Ted.

Soon Henry's bag was stuffed
with treats.

Ding dong.

Horrid Henry opened the door.

"Boo," said Atomic Bunny.

Henry's sweet bag!
Help! Mum would see it!

"Eeeeek!"

screeched Horrid Henry.
"Help! Save me!"

Quickly, he ran upstairs
clutching his bag and hid it
safely under his bed.

Phew, that was close.

"Don't be scared, Henry,
it's only me," called Perfect Peter.

Horrid Henry came back downstairs.

"No!" said Henry.
"I'd never have known."

"Really?" said Peter.

"Really," said Henry.

"Everyone just gave sweets
this year," said Perfect Peter.

"Yuck."

Horrid Henry held out the lucky dip.

"Ooh, a satsuma," said Peter.
"Aren't I lucky?"

"I hope you've learned your lesson,
Henry," said Mum sternly.

"I certainly have,"
said Horrid Henry, eyeing
Perfect Peter's bulging bag.
"Good things come to those
who wait."

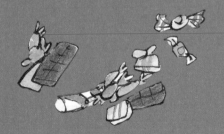